Hero Mom

by **Melinda Hardin**
illustrated by **Bryan Langdo**

Amazon Children's Publishing

Text copyright © 2013 by Melinda Hardin
Illustrations copyright © 2013 by Bryan Langdo

Amazon Publishing
Attn: Amazon Children's Publishing
P.O. Box 400818
Las Vegas, NV 89140
www.amazon.com/amazonchildrenspublishing

Printed in China (R)
First edition, 2013
10 9 8 7 6 5 4 3 2 1.

ISBN-13: 9781477816455 (hardcover)
ISBN-10: 1477816453 (hardcover)
ISBN-13: 9781477866450 (eBook)
ISBN-10: 1477866450 (eBook)

The illustrations are rendered in Windsor & Newton
watercolors on Fabriano Artistico watercolor paper.

Book design by Vera Soki
Editor: Marilyn Brigham

For Lilly and Alden
 —*M.H.*

For the mom of my kids. You are their hero.
 —*B.L.*

Our moms are superheroes.

My mom doesn't fly in to save the day—
well, sometimes she does.

My mom doesn't command animals—
she works with them to find missing
people and dangerous objects.

My mom can't transform into a machine, but she can make airplanes fly, trucks run, and tanks roll.

My mom doesn't have super-human speed, but she gets everything where it needs to go, just in time.

My mom doesn't have
super-healing powers—
well, maybe she does.

My mom doesn't lead a band of superheroes—
she leads a battalion.

Even though our moms go away on long trips, we feel their super love for us in their letters, pictures, and phone calls.

Our moms are
American Soldiers.

Our moms are heroes.
Our superheroes.